I0624240

Other Books by Eric Krimmel

15 Moments

The Cross Country Adventures of the
Blue Highways Cycling Elite

Illuminate: The yearlong photo-a-day project

Uncut Garden

www.erickrimmel.com

Copyright

www.erickrimmel.com

Jimland

Eric Krimmel

Acknowledgements

I wish to express my thanks to Ann Cook, Elizabeth Krimmel, Anita O'Brien and Alexandre Strube for their assistance in editing this work.

www.erickrimmel.com

Jimland

Eric Krimmel

1

"*Where* are you going?" Megan asked.

Jill and Megan were having lunch in a small diner with big windows overlooking the bustle of the city. Jill was easing into a conversation about her vacation plans but was unsure how to tell her friend about it.

"To Jim."

"That doesn't sound like a place, it sounds like a guy's name."

"It is."

"What?"

"I'm not going to a geographical place as much as I'm taking a trip back to the old relationship I had with Jim."

"Oh." She looked at her friend as if trying to figure out what she just said. "What?"

After relieving the tension of telling Megan her plan, Jill became more animated knowing she would have a hard time selling this idea to her best friend.

"I know this is going to sound crazy but I've been casually thinking about where I was going to go on vacation. I figured we'd do something together but that wouldn't use up all of my vacation time and I wasn't all that excited about any of the other ideas I had come up with. A great trip isn't so much about going somewhere, as it's about who you go with and what you do– something adventurous, something different. That's when I heard from Jim. You remember, he's the guy I broke up with just after we met."

"What I remember is you complaining about him a lot."

"Yeah, I'm sure I didn't have a lot of good things to say about him then. I loved him, but I realized I couldn't be with a guy like that and I don't think he wanted to get married, ever, to me or anyone. You remember, it was a hard break up."

"So he just called you out of the blue, after, like, a year?"

"Yeah, said he was thinking about me. It was great to hear from him, we must have talked for 3 hours."

"And just like that, you're flying out to see him? Because that is crazy."

"No. He wanted to come here for a weekend and I told him I was going on vacation. He said he'd meet me, just pick a spot."

"So you are going to meet him somewhere? Still crazy."

"Yes, I'm meeting him somewhere. No, it's not crazy. It's not a typical vacation in that I'm going to a location on a map, but I am going somewhere special, a place where I really enjoyed myself, where I was happy."

"You obviously weren't that happy or you would still be together. This is a bad idea."

"It isn't. There are reasons we broke up and I understand why we're not together. But this way I get all the good stuff from a relationship without all the bad and mundane garbage. I get the fun, the romance, the laughter, without the fights– we won't be together long enough to let the little things get to us. Or the mundane things like having to cook for him or nag him to cut the grass, or put down the toilet seat, or having to watch a dumb movie I didn't want to see in the first place."

"A relationship is a bit more complicated than that."

"Right, but this isn't going to be a relationship, it's just a visit to a relationship. It's like pretending we're in a relationship without actually being in one."

"Is this a joke?"

"Not at all! I'm going to a place I love, the good part of an old relationship, and it's the perfect vacation. I'm doing something different, something adventurous, with someone special and when it's over I'll be ready to come home."

"What if you fall for him again? Or what if he falls for you?"

"I won't fall for him, I know why we broke up. Sure I think, What if? sometimes, but it's always what if Jim were different in many ways. Even if he changed a little he would never change that

8

much. Jim is a good guy, but in this respect he's like a lot of other people, he doesn't think his bad qualities are really that bad, so he has no incentive to change. He thought it was always me who had to get over it. For as much as I liked him that's not the person I want to be with. Now, if he wants something more, I'll just tell him no."

"Just like that, huh?"

"Well, I'm not 18 anymore, so the idea that the person I'm most attracted to will magically have all the qualities I'm looking for is a thing of the past. But I'm not 28 anymore either, so after a few relationships and too many dates, I'm pretty sure I know what I'm looking for without being unrealistic. It's nice that he's handsome, has a nice body, is charming and sexy, we have a lot in common… but no, it's not enough to sustain a relationship."

"Ooookay," Megan said in a mocking manner. "It just doesn't sound like it's going to be that easy. What happens when you come back, when the vacation is over? Are you going to be able to let go?"

"Of course! Think about it this way, you love Spain. You always have a great time there. When you get back do you feel that you have to give up everything you have here and move to Spain?"

"I've considered it."

"Why didn't you do it? You've been there a number of times. And each time you come home you are happy you went, a little sad the trip didn't last a bit longer, but have decided your life is here. The same is true with Jim. It's a nice place to visit but, as much as I like it, all things considered, I don't want to live in Jimland."

"That sounds logical, but it still doesn't make a lot of sense. Are you sure you want to do this?"

"Yes. I leave on Saturday and I'll tell you all about it when I get back. Because I'm not taking my phone either."

"Oh, this idea just keeps getting crazier."

"There's nothing crazy about this! I'm going on vacation, completely forget about my regular life, relax," then with a smile on her face, "have my needs attended to, and come back a new woman. This is the best idea I ever had!"

2

It was early evening when Jill walked into her apartment, went straight to the bedroom and plopped her suitcase on the bed. She threw her coat on the chair and grabbed her phone off of the bedside table. She scrolled through messages looking for anything crucial, then dialed Megan's number.

"Oh thank god you're safe!"

"Oh Megan, don't be so melodramatic. Of course I'm safe, and the trip was great! Hurry over and I'll tell you all about it!"

"So it was good, seeing Jim again?"

"Oh yeah! Fantastic! C'mon over and I'll give you all the details."

"I'll be right there!"

15 minutes later the door bell rings, Jill races to the door, wildly pulls it open and throws her arms around Megan.

"I missed you!"

"I missed you, too!"

Jill lets go, pulls back and thrusts the back of her left hand into Megan's face. "Look! We got married!"

Megan stood perfectly still, mouth open, conflicted over whether to shout congratulations or reach out and slap Jill in the face for being so stupid.

Jill starts cooing, "Oh my god, I forgot how dreamy he is." She tilted her head slightly to the side, then rolled her eyes upward like a teenager talking about her first crush.

"He met me at the airport and when I saw him I just knew this was going to be the best vacation I ever had. He was wearing this blue sweater that reminded me of the first time we met. He walked over, wrapped his arms around me and picked me right up off the ground. I was breathless."

Jill spun around, walked into the living room and plopped down on the couch. Megan stiffly walked to a chair across from Jill as if her legs were the only part of her body she could move. She slowly sat down.

"The first week we saw all the top sights: the Eiffel Tower, the Arc de Triumph, the Louvre, the Musee D'orsey, everything! We ate in small restaurants and had breakfast in outdoor cafes. It was great! And now I'm moving to California!"

Jill went on to describe the trip in more detail but Megan couldn't hear a word, her head was swimming, unable to focus. Suddenly she snapped back to reality.

"I asked, 'Aren't you happy for me?'"

"This is what I said was going to happen."

"No it isn't."

"Remember the analogy you used about me going to Spain, and in spite of loving it, returning to my normal life? This is like going to Spain and buying the country!"

"Oh that's just ridiculous."

"That's my point!"

"There is nothing ridiculous about this."

Meagan looked at Jill with the utmost disbelief. "Are you insane?"

"Why can't you just be happy for me!"

Megan exhaled loudly. "I need some wine."

"Fine." Jill marched off into the kitchen to open a bottle and get some glasses. She came back and poured out the wine. She handed Megan a glass and before she could sit down, Megan gulped half of it.

"A toast?" Jill said raising her glass.

"To sanity," and then Megan finished the glass.

"Not funny."

Megan put her elbows on her knees and took a couple of deep breaths. "Are you sure this is the guy for you?"

"Yes. It feels right. It feels like I did the right thing. I'm happy."

Megan let herself plop back into the chair and folded her arms across her chest. "But this is the guy you had to break up with. The guy you complained about repeatedly. The guy who, you, logically explained to me, wasn't the guy for you. Doesn't that matter?"

"No." She paused for a second then said, "I don't know. Does anyone really know?"

"Oh, god."

"It seems like everyone is looking for perfection and they justify that by saying they won't settle. Perfection doesn't exist. You can have a great relationship with a man you don't always agree with, you don't have to have everything in common. If you are committed to working out your differences, the things that make each other crazy, and love each other, isn't everything else a bonus?"

"What about having some fun? Having your needs attended to? What happened to miss smarty pants who was too brilliant to get trapped by a boorish man?"

"Well, Jim isn't boorish so I guess I am pretty smart after all."

"But even if you wanted to start seeing him again how could you decide to get engaged and married in just two weeks?"

"If you know he's the right guy, why waste time? Most couples have a long courtship and engagement but the divorce rate is still pretty high so I guess that system isn't foolproof, is it?"

"I can't believe this."

There was an awkward silence. "I'm disappointed you're not happy for me."

Megan sighed, "You're my best friend, and I don't want to offend you, but I can't help but think you are ruining your life."

"I'm not. Megan, Jim is a great guy. Besides, I was ready for a change. I have a couple close friends here in Chicago but none of my family is here. I don't own a house or much stuff, I'm not friends with any of my neighbors. I've felt stuck in my job without a real chance to advance. What is the worst thing that could happen? If it doesn't work out, we get a divorce, and I can move back."

Megan was unconvinced. "But what about going on vacation, having some fun, then coming back. I haven't moved to Spain."

"The reason you don't move to Spain is because your life is good. My life wasn't that great."

Megan looked away and wiped a few tears from her eyes. "More wine."

Jill poured out the rest of the bottle.

"If you are really happy, if this is what you want, then I'm happy for you." Megan half-heartedly raised her glass a few inches, "A toast, to you and Jim. Congratulations."

"Thanks."

Megan got up and walked over to sit next to Jill on the couch. "I'm really going to miss you."

"I'm going to miss you, too. Which is why I want you to come to California with me for a few days."

"What?"

"I want you to take some time off and come to California with me, to help me settle in. You helped me pick out nearly everything I bought when I redid my place and we had so much fun doing it. I'm sure his place will need to be redecorated so I'll need some help shopping and we'll be able to spend a lot of time together before we have to say good bye."

Megan just stared at her.

"Well, what do you say?"

"I think that is probably the only thing you've said since I got here that doesn't sound crazy."

Jill laughed and said, "Good. This is going to be so much fun!"

3

It's Monday morning and I'm pouring myself a cup of coffee in the open kitchenette just inside the door of my division. I run the small graphic design department of a software company. My employees and I line a wall in a massive room with an open-office floor plan that is shared with the sales and support staff and programmers. A steady stream of coworkers file in as I acknowledge them.

"Tom," I say and nod. Tom nods back.

"Rebecca."

"Good morning."

I add a little milk to my coffee. "Saul."

Saul, winks and points at me. I smile. The men here are certainly more playful than the women. Maybe the women are just more concerned that a such behavior might be misconstrued as flirtatious. I add half a teaspoon of sugar.

"There he is, the Sales-inator, three time winner of the Salesperson of the Year award."

"The one and only, and I feel like a billion bucks."

"Don't rub it in. It'll be a while before I can enjoy some R&R. Have a good time?"

"Yeah." He walks up to the counter and grabs a cup. "What's been going on here for the past two weeks?"

"Nothing unusual. They had a big meeting with R.K.S. and I guess there are some additions to their contract, that's about it. Jonah didn't mess up your accounts too bad, but I did hear that Traruba had an issue and it took him three days to figure it out."

"Oh, great. They're not pissed I was unavailable?"

"No, I think after everything was worked out, they were fine."

We start to walk back toward our desks. "What about your vacation? I had that business trip and when I came back you were gone. That was kind of spur of the moment."

"Yeah, something came together at the last second."

"Where did you go?"

"I went to Paris."

"Really? Paris?"

"Yup."

"Don't you usually go to a place with plenty of booze and bikinis?"

"Changed it up. New man."

"Did you have fun?"

"Yeah, it was ok, I mean it's in France, so, you know. There are a lot of things not to like about a foreign country. It's so irritating they speak a different language."

"What did you do when you where there?"

"Saw most of the top sites. Got married."

"What?"

"You know the Eiffel Tower, the—"

"No. The married part."

"Yeah. Got married."

"I didn't know you were engaged."

"I wasn't. Well, I was for about three days."

"What?"

"I figured it was time. I want to have kids. All my brothers are settled down, most of my friends. I've known some women in my time," then in a low voice while tilting his head forward and talking out of the side of his mouth, says, "banged some hot chicks," then straightens up, shrugs and says, "so I opened the little black book and picked the best one."

"And just like that, she said yes?"

"Well, not exactly. I got my third choice. But she's hot; nice body, pretty face. I don't like her hair and the way she dresses sometimes makes her look like her mom, but it's good."

If anyone else were telling me this I'd know it was a joke but with Jim it was entirely possible. "Are you serious?"

Jim held up his hand to show me his gold wedding band. Yes, when I took a second to think about it, this was extreme but I shouldn't have been that surprised.

"She lives in Chicago and she's packing up her stuff and moving out here. I don't know where I'm going to put it all. I told her not to bring too much of her crap."

I smiled, "And she was ok with that?"

"Well, we don't need two beds, two sofas, more than two recliners. I told her if she had some kitchen stuff that would be good because if I'm not eating out…" Jim paused and a wry smile crossed his face, "I mean food, so get your mind out of the gutter…"

"Yeah I get it," and think, sarcastically, No Jim, your high school humor never gets old.

"…I'm just going to order pizza, or heat up some soup and make some nachos. So she's going to need some cooking stuff."

We were still standing in the isle near our desks when the manager of Sales and Support, walks up, looks at Jim, and in a monotone voice says, "Jim."

"Pete. What's up?"

"Good vacation?"

"Yeah."

"Good. There have been some changes to the R.K.S. account. I need you to get up to speed on those." He hands Jim a file folder.

"Sure, I'll get right on it."

Pete walks away.

"This is odd, getting married like this. How much do you know about this woman?"

"We were in a relationship for about a year and then we broke up for some reason. I can't remember."

Be-do-beep. Jim reaches down and unclips his cell phone from his belt. A text, Thinking of you, with a smiley face emoticon. Jim smiles, shows me, "From the wife," then texts, Me too, and sends it. "Oops." He sends another text of a smiley face and clips his phone back on his belt.

A second later, be-do-beep. "Oh, jeez. It's starting already." He reads it and then says, "Hey, I better get on these changes," referring to his account.

"You're not going to fill me in?"

"About what?"

"We'll talk at lunch."

An hour or so into changing figures on dozens of spreadsheets, reviewing contract terms on the R.K.S account and numerous texts from Jill, Jim's phone rings. He has a habit of answering on speaker phone so those in close proximity can hear his conversations.

"Hey how was your vacation?" It was his brother.

"Good. Let me ask you a question. Does Deb text you all the time?"

"Well, some days she texts a lot."

"Man! Isn't that annoying?"

"What?"

"When your wife won't stop texting you."

"Ah, yes."

"This is so great. Now we can bitch about our wives together."

"What?"

"Oh, I guess I forgot to tell you. I got married."

"What?"

"Yeah, it's no big deal."

"Oh no, it's a real big deal. When did this happen?"

"Last week."

"Does mom and dad know?"

"I haven't talked to them since I got back so I guess not."

"You have to call them immediately and tell them."

"I'll give them a call tonight."

"No, right now."

"Steve, did I ever tell you that I never grow tired of my older brother telling me what to do?"

"And how many times have I saved your butt with my advice?"

"Maybe once."

"Don't make me make a list! This is a big deal and you don't want to hurt mom and dad."

"They're not going to be hurt. They've been wanting me to settle down for a long time now."

"It's not that they'll be upset because you're married, it's because you did it and didn't tell, or invite them. Call them now."

"Hey, they're retired, they might be enjoying some, *afternoon delight*. Except it's not even noon so I guess that would be morning delight. Or how about brunch delight? Maybe they're *eating out.*"

"Thank you for that image of our parents! Even if they are... *busy*, you have to call them right away."

Be-do-beep. "I'm getting a text from the old lady. Women! Know what I'm saying? Got to go." He hangs up and looks at the text. "Clothes packed. Kitchen utensils and appliances next," Jim reads out loud. "I really don't need a play by play."

My work station is right across from Jim's and I can hear everything he's saying as if he's purposely narrating his life.

I spin my chair around and look across the isle, "Time of your life, buddy!" and chuckle. "This may be the smartest thing you've ever done."

Jim shoots me a halfhearted smile and sets his phone on the desk then turns toward his computer.

"Oh, and that thing about calling everybody to tell them you're married? That's such a hassle. Just update your status on Facebook and send out a tweet. That's how people do it now," I said in jest.

Both Jim and I were lost in the current projects we were working on when Jim cranes his neck around and says to me, "It's 12:35, do you want to head to Medici?"

"Yeah, give me two minutes."

On the ride over Jim talks about a mess he's been working on all morning. When we are seated and order, he concludes with, "So anyway, now we just have to code the new features."

"Now tell me about your trip."

"Not much to tell. I got there about an hour before she arrived–"

"Just for the sake of clarity, you went to Paris?"

"Yeah."

"The real Paris. Paris, France. Not Paris, Texas?"

"Cute. The real one. It was her idea."

"So I walked over to the bar and got a couple of drinks and checked my email. Then I headed to the gate and when she saw me she practically ran up to me. When I hugged her I picked her right up off the ground, I forgot how short she was."

"Then?" I said.

Jim shrugged. "We did a bunch of sightseeing, you know, the

18

tourist stuff, and we had a good time. When she first asked me to meet her in Paris I thought it was going to blow. No beach, no endless supply of alcohol while lying in the sun. But it was good."

I knew Jim was impulsive but I was having a hard time accepting his nonchalance about something as important as this. "When you said you just opened your little black book and picked a woman, you were joking, right?"

"There are a handful of women that I've dated for more than a couple of months. I figured that my best chance for a relationship had to be with one of them. In each case it was a mutual decision to break up so if I was willing to get over some things to make it work, then she should be too."

"How long has it been since you guys broke up?"

"About a year."

"But you've kept in touch with her and have seen her since, right?"

"No. I hadn't talked to her since. I called her up and we talked for a really long time then she asked me to meet her in Paris. I wasn't planning on proposing right away but we were having such a good time I figured, why not? I got up early one day and told her I was going for coffee. I had noticed there was a jewelry store near our hotel. I picked out a nice, simple ring and thought if she said yes we could pick out a wedding band together."

I asked about the proposal knowing how important this event is to women. I was anticipating anything from, 'Here, I got this for you, what do you think?' as she stepped out of the shower, to putting the ring in a milkshake bought from a fast food chain and then getting upset when she didn't find it and tossed the last of the milkshake in the trash. I imagined Jim pulling the container out of the trash, extracting the goop-covered ring and yelling at her for not finding it, to which an appropriate response would be, "What idiot puts an engagement ring in the bottom of a milkshake?"

"I googled it."

"What?"

"I googled, How to propose marriage if you are in Paris. I picked one that sounded good. It was easy, and besides, chicks dig that stuff."

Surprised, I asked, "How did it go?"

"That afternoon she had something else planned but I called an audible. I figured I might as well go for it. There's a place, I can't remember the name, that's the highest point in Paris. We went in the evening when the sun was low and everything was turning that golden hue. The Eiffel Tower is right there, the city is spread out before you, and boom, I popped the question. We stayed until after sunset to see Paris all lit up."

"You mean the Basilique de Sacre-Coeur?"

"I don't know, all those French words sound alike to me. Besides, as proposals go, how is anyone going to top Paris? I win!"

I was amazed. "It certainly is an impressive story." There are things in which Jim appeared clueless, but then he does something like this. "And your marriage license is valid here?"

"What?"

"If you get married outside the United States does the government still recognize it here?"

"Don't know, didn't think about it. But if Jill isn't the one, it might be a way out."

And he's back. That's the Jim I know.

Later in the afternoon Jim gets up and walks across the aisle to my work station. "Jill has been texting me all day about packing up her stuff and it sounds like she has a mountain of things she's bringing. I'm going to have to rent a storage unit."

"For your stuff?"

"Hardly. I don't want her to be bringing any girly crap into my house."

"You do understand that it's no longer your house?"

"What?"

"Don't worry, you'll get it in about a week or so."

"I'm just saying that a recliner, a real one, only comes in brown or black and is made of leather. You know they make those girly versions now. They're smaller and come with floral fabric? Eech." He made a face that looked like a kid eating spinach.

"I'm sure she doesn't have one of those."

"How do you know?"

"The only people who have those are married people. They're

what couples buy as a compromise. Single women don't buy those and single men don't buy them either."

"Good, because I don't want to give up any of my stuff."

I laughed.

"What?"

"Oh, it's hard to explain, but you'll understand once she gets here."

"That will be Wednesday. Hey, you should come over to meet her."

I was curious to see the woman who would marry Jim, and do so on the spur of the moment.

"If you stop by after work we'll be there. I'm taking the day off, cleaning up the place. The movers will be here on Friday and Jill wants to paint and decorate a bit. I told her it was ok, but no girl colors. I'm not living in a house with pink walls."

Smiling I said, "Yeah, that sounds good."

4

I was running back and forth all day to a small room where our printers were spitting out comps for a series of magazine ads we were running soon. I was at my desk when Jim walked across the aisle about 4:00, ready to leave.

"I'm taking off. So you're coming over tomorrow, to meet Jill?"

"Yeah, what time?"

"Her flight gets in at 2:00, she's getting a rental because her car won't be here for a few days, so she's driving to the house. Around 3:00. And she's bringing her hot friend, I'll hook you up." Jim was smiling.

"No! Don't do that! Really, I can't endure another blind date."

"Ok, ok. She'll be there and if you like her you can hit on her, if not, no big deal."

"That's best."

Jim was still standing there, smiling.

"What?"

"I don't know if she's hot. I haven't met her, I haven't even seen a picture of her."

"So you were going to fix me up with some obnoxious, ugly chick?"

"Maybe." We both chuckled. "What's the big deal? Don't you get a free set of steak knives if you go on one more bad date?"

"That would be little consolation."

"I still think you should ask Rachel out."

"Sssh!" I said glancing toward her desk. "First, I'm like 15 years older than she is and second, I'm her boss and that might be considered sexual harassment, not to mention there is a company policy against it."

"Eight."

"What?"

"She's eight years younger."

"You know her age?"

"Sure," Jim said with a shrug. "I asked her. So, if you don't tell her about your false teeth and cane I think you'll be fine, grandpa. You might even score."

"Stop."

"I see the way see looks at you."

"It's not going to happen. Even if she is interested I'm not going to risk my job for a date."

"No one has to know."

"You can't keep stuff like that a secret. Everyone here knew Doug was having an affair six months before his wife did. Patterson? From accounting? Slept with a hooker when he was out of town at a convention, and everybody knows about that."

Jim put his hands in the air, palms out, about shoulder high, "Ok. Well, maybe Jill's friend will work out for you." He lowered his hands.

"With my luck over the past couple of years, I'm not holding my breath. Oh, that reminds me, you should get some flowers for Jill for when she gets here."

"Why? We're not courting, I already got her."

"Let me put this in Jim-terms. Happy wife, good sex. Unhappy wife, no sex. And now that you're married you can't open the little black book or wait around at a bar until 2:00 a.m. to pick up what's left over if you're not getting any."

"You are a smart man."

"But hey, not as smart as you since I haven't been able to convince a woman to marry me," I said with a smile on my face.

"So true, buddy, so true."

5

It had been a late night at the office for the last couple of days but now that things settled down I was planning on leaving early. By the time I wrapped up what needed to be done, I realized I could make it to Jim's just about the time Jill and her friend would be arriving.

I show up at Jim's and he answers the door. "Hey buddy, glad you could stop by. What do you say to a beer?"

"Where have you been my whole life, gorgeous?"

Jim smiles, "That joke never gets old."

"Oh, it was old decades ago. But I know you like it."

"You're a pal."

Jim goes into the kitchen to get the drinks. He comes out and tosses me a beer.

"Was their flight on time?"

"Yeah, I just talked to her and they'll be here soon. I want to show you something awesome in the backyard. C'mon."

In my mind I start guessing. 10 foot long grill? The neighbor's young wife in a bikini, sunbathing? A giant banner, ode to his favorite team the Detroit Tigers? He would frequently say, "You know I grew up in Detroit. Well, the suburbs." and "My favorite Tiger of all time? Hank Greenberg. You thought I was going to say Ty Cobb. Cobb was a dirty player. I can't admire a guy like that."

We get out into the yard and Jim says, "Look at the size of those tomatoes."

A lot of what Jim said sounded like a sexual innuendo, because a good percentage was sexual innuendo, but in this case he was actually referring to impressive four foot tall tomato plants with large tomatoes hanging from them.

"Wow, those are nice."

Jim starts in with soil composition and leads me through proper hydration, pruning, different varieties and subtle nuances of flavor, then ends with, "I don't know what it is but I just really love a good tomato. And you can't get anything fresher than pulling it off the vine just before you slice it up."

"Absolutely."

"Let me find a good ripe one. I've got some chicken salad in the house and I'll make us some sandwiches."

"You don't have to go to any trouble."

"It'll take a second."

We head back into the house and Jim starts pulling food out of the refrigerator. A couple of minutes later I take the first juicy bite. "Excellent. Good job."

"Thanks. I got the chicken salad from the little deli down the road. Organic, free range. If I eat healthy some of the time I don't have to feel guilty about eating junk some times. I'm not 20 years old anymore and I've got to start thinking about this stuff."

Half way through our sandwiches, be-do-beep. Jim grabs his phone, smiles and says, "They're on Eliot." He starts typing while narrating out loud, "Second light about 1 mile. Turn right. 4th from the corner on left. 1832." He looks up at me and says, "You can't always trust GPS."

Jim sets his phone down and devours the rest of his sandwich.

"Another brewski?"

"No, I'm good."

Jim started cleaning up, washing the few dishes that were dirty and wiping everything down. He was clearly nervous, or excited, or something. I've never seen him like this. He could make a presentation when a $10 million account was in the balance and not even flinch, so this was unusual.

"Relax."

"What?"

"You just seem a little uptight."

"I don't get uptight."

A few minutes later, the door bell rings, Jim answers and Jill jumps into his arms. I have to admit they truly looked happy to see each other. Still, I couldn't help but think, "Crazy, meet crazy."

Jim asked her about the trip but I wasn't paying attention. Jill's friend walked in behind her and was standing there like a little girl waiting to be acknowledged. She was very attractive, looked over at me and I smiled. She returned a half smile then looked away.

"Oh, this is Megan," Jill said spinning around and pushing Megan toward Jim.

"It's nice to meet you," Jim said as he extended his hand. "This is where I would say I've heard so much about you. But I haven't. Barely anything."

Then Jim introduced me to Jill and she walked over and threw her arms around me, "I'm glad to meet you!" She hugged me hard as if she was trying to squeeze the air out of me. I hugged her back.

"Hey, no groping my wife, buddy."

Jill released me and said, "Oh, Jim." We were all smiling except Megan. Jill then said, "And this is Megan." I extended my hand and she shook it.

"It's nice to meet you," I said.

"It's nice to meet you."

"Hey, I got you these flowers for you," Jim said to Jill. He walked over to the dining room table to get them.

"Oh, they're lovely! Thank you!"

Jim blurted out that it was my idea. "He's a good wing man."

No, he did not just say that, I thought. You are not going to score any points that way. I look at Jim with a slight frown on my face.

He looks at Jill and says, "But he won't have to remind me in the future."

"Awww…"

What? What just happened? I mouthed, Good save, to Jim behind Jill's back. Jim gave a slight nod of the head to acknowledge it.

"Well, this is mi casa. Let me show you around."

Jill looked past the living room to the patio doors and said, "It looks like you have a nice yard."

"Ok, let's start there." We walked outside. Jim lead Jill straight back to the tomatoes so he could show them off again.

I turned to Megan, "I've already been on the tomato tour, but

Jim's admiration of the fruit is quite fascinating if you want to catch up."

"I'm ok, thanks."

"How long have you known Jill?"

"For a while."

"Jim and I work together."

"I figured it was something like that."

She's seems nice, probably just shy, I thought. After a few days, she'll be more talkative.

Jim lead Jill back into the house. I waited for Megan to follow and she slowly walked in that direction but stopped before she stepped inside and waited until Jim and Jill were out of sight, then turned to me and unleashed a fury.

"So you're the guy who put Jim up to this?"

"What?"

"How could you let this happen?"

"Ah…"

"You think this is funny? You think this is a joke? Did you put him up to marrying Jill, because this is clearly the worst thing that ever happened to my best friend and I think I might kill you!"

"What? No! I found out the day he came back to work. I had no idea this was going on or that he had asked two other women first."

"Jill was his third choice?" She screamed in a harsh whisper. Megan's head looked like it was about to explode.

"Why are you so upset?"

"Your jerky buddy stole my best friend! This is the worst thing that has ever happened to her and I blame you!"

Jill stuck her head around the open patio door. "Hey guys, how are you doing?"

Megan turned toward her, "Great," and walked into the house.

Jill lead us down the hall toward the bedrooms. She walked past the first one, "This is our room," and when she came to the second one, "This is your room, Megan."

Jim was standing there and said to me, "Help me with the suitcases."

"Sure." We walked outside toward the rental car.

"So, what about Megan? She's pretty hot. You should have let me fix you up."

"Oh, yeah, she's attractive alright."

"So?"

In a low mumble I said, "I'm trying to break my streak of dating psychotic women."

"What?"

"We're getting to know each other," I said in a louder voice. I wasn't sure if calling Megan certifiably crazy would create an issue for Jim or not. But I also thought it might be more fun if he found out himself, since he wanted to fix me up with her before he knew anything about her, so I held back. We walked into the house with the luggage.

"Those are Megan's." Jim turned into his bedroom and Jill was standing inside. I paused, then reluctantly walked down the hall. Megan was sitting on the bed with her arms folded across her chest, staring at the floor. I plopped the suitcases on the end of the bed with the idea of making a quick exit when Megan got up, blocked the doorway and came at me again.

"And you're the one who told him that the proper way to tell your family and closest friends that you just got married is to post it on Facebook?"

"Well…"

"Are you insane?"

"I was just playing with him! It was a joke!"

"Real funny. You think this is a game? What was the strategy here? How did you convince Jim to propose? I'm sure all of you guys got a big laugh out of it! What a bunch of jerks!"

Without knocking her out of the way I couldn't escape so I needed to push back.

"Whoa, girl! There wasn't any kind of conspiracy. No one knew he was even thinking about this, not even his brothers. In fact, I would hardly say that anything Jim does outside work comes from a plan. At least not a well thought out one."

Before she could say anything, I added, "And correct me if I'm wrong but going to Paris was Jill's idea, not Jim's, and she invited him not the other way around. In fact, if we're concocting crazy conspiracy theories, it sounds like you, Jill, and some of those pathetic, How To Snag a Husband, books laid out a carefully crafted Man Trap!"

"Wrong! I told Jill this was the craziest thing she ever thought of. I told her not to do it! And if Jill was looking to manipulate Jim she would have had him meet her in some tropical place where she'd be wearing a bikini all day long because all you have to do is show a man some skin suddenly he can't think straight!"

"Oh that's just not true." Actually, it is so true. Well, a little true.

I needed to get out of there. "This is ridiculous," I said as I squeezed past Megan and out the bedroom door. I walked down the hall and stuck my head in Jim's bedroom. Jill and Jim were sitting on the bed. "Hey, I'm sure the girls are tired after the long flight and I've got some work to do before tomorrow. It was nice meeting you, Jill, and I'll see you tomorrow at the office," I said to Jim.

"We were talking about going to get something to eat. Come with us."

"Some other time, I really have to go. Just stay here, I can see myself out."

"Ok. Tomorrow."

"See you then."

"It was nice meeting you!" Jill yelled after me as I turned to leave. I walked out the front door and as I made my way to the car, thought, They're all nuts. Just get in your car and drive far, far away.

6

"Who was number one?"

"Maria." Jim and I were sitting in the lunchroom at work the next day.

"Maria. Maria?"

"She has some issues."

"You were in Macy's, she had a melt down and started throwing plates at you. She busted up some displays and was arrested."

"She's a little emotional."

"She's a psycho! And that was your first choice?"

"I don't know, there's just something about her." Jim tried to think of what it was. "I don't know what I was thinking." Jim took another bite of his sandwich and stared off into space. "Yes I do. In the bedroom, that kind of passion…" Jim's voice trailed off as a smile crossed his face.

"And outside the bedroom?"

Jim snapped back from his daydream, blinked his eyes a few times and without moving his head looked at me, "Not good."

"The big question is, did you really want to be married to her?"

"I had just started thinking about this whole marriage thing. For a long time I resisted even the idea of it without much thought. But the more I considered it, the more I was convinced that this was the direction I wanted to take my life in. I'm in a good position now: good job, nice house, money in the bank. The hunt, the pursuit, always has a sense of thrill to it, but too often it seems like you're running down a blind alley that dead ends, even when you score. I guess that I had thought about it long enough to think, I'm ready, let's just get it done."

"But Maria?"

"No, I don't know what I was thinking. It just seemed like a good idea at the time. I guess I dodged a bullet." Jim took another bite of his sandwich. "And when she said no, she didn't even throw anything at me."

We laughed.

"You know you are in a bad relationship when you say things like, 'And she didn't even throw a plate at my head this time.'"

I couldn't believe Jim picked someone, proposed, and got married in less than a month. "It all happened pretty fast, was that the plan all along?"

"Not really. I figured I'd pick someone, we'd hang out for a while just so I could be sure and then I'd ask her. I really didn't know how long that might be. But Maria, she saw right through me. She wanted to know what was going on right away. I never could get away with anything with her. It was really irritating. But also, in a way, very comforting. I never had to worry, Oh, she's not going to like it when she finds out… because if I tried to pull anything over on her, she was on top of it. It sounds like a bad thing, and there were times when I was upset about it, but it was great."

"What about number two?"

"She was a long shot and I knew it but I had to contact her just for peace of mind. We were in a relationship a long time ago. I was crazy about her. She often became irritated with me for little things. She would make a big deal out of me wearing a hat or shirt she didn't like, so of course I did it all the time. I thought it was funny when she got mad. She didn't. She was just so cute. I'd do something she didn't like, she would get mad and then I'd make it worse because I'd laugh or smile when she got mad. Now I can see it was pretty childish, but then it just seemed so endearing."

"So what happened?"

"After a while it became irritating. It was like she couldn't accept me for who I was, like she was trying to turn me into her ideal man. Eventually it just seemed like she was criticizing everything I did. When I'd think about her, after we broke up, I'd wonder if we were simply too young. It was my first serious relationship. Hers, too. I would see her now and again over the years, but she was always with someone else."

"What happened when you got a hold of her?"

"We had a long talk. I brought up the things that used to bother her. It seems like I've grown since that time and she hasn't. But it doesn't matter. She's engaged."

"Do you think you would have been happy with her?"

"After we had that talk, no. But I think I needed to do it, just to be sure."

"So Jill was the right one."

"Yeah, without a doubt. Once I saw her, and we spent some time together, I just knew. I don't know how, but I knew."

Across town, at Jim's house, Jill and Megan were halfway into painting the dining and living room. Up to this point Jill was doing all of the talking, but for the last 15 minutes they worked in silence.

"I can't stand this. You have to tell me what's wrong. Do you hate me? Do you hate Jim? Was it a bad idea to ask you to help me? We had such a good time redecorating my place," Jill said.

"No! No."

"Then what is it. You've been quiet and mopey since we got here."

Megan sighed and stopped painting. She was stooped down cutting in the wall just above the baseboard and rocked back so that she could sit on the floor. She set down the brush and turned toward Jill, who was on the ladder rolling out the wall near the ceiling. "It just seems like there was a lot more to take in than I thought."

"The decorating? I'm sorry, I should have been less ambitious."

"No. His place needs it. It's this whole situation, between you and Jim."

"Yeah, I kind of dropped it on you like a bomb. I'm sorry."

"Well, yeah. When you told me you got married and then right after that, you were moving, it was a shock. But eventually I realized that it was selfish to be sad that I was losing a friend to hang out with if you were happy, because that's what's important. Still, I couldn't shake this feeling of… disappointment."

"Disappointment?"

"Yeah, I've been thinking about this since we got here. There are some things I didn't see right away."

"Like what?"

"First, it reminded me that I'm not getting any younger and haven't had good luck with relationships myself."

"Oh! You'll find someone! Don't worry!" Jill set down the roller and climbed off the ladder to sit next to Megan on the floor.

"Yeah, I know. I'm not in a panic about it or anything but I feel like you moved on with your life and I haven't. But that's ok, and I'm fine with that. I've been working on my career and haven't spent much time dating. Prince Charming didn't fall in my lap so I just have to put more effort into it, if that's what I want. But there's more."

"What else?"

"You know when you first start to date a guy and get to know him? All the little stories about the cute things he does and the dumb things he does and his little habits and how the relationship is going and how he compares to the other guys you dated and the guys your friends dated and all that? You skipped that. Then, as things get more serious, the anticipation of the proposal and trying to guess when and how he'll do it, and what the ring will look like, then planning the wedding and trying on dresses and where you are going to have it and picking out the cake... we didn't get a chance to share any of that. And now it's too late."

"Oh! I never thought about that! I feel so bad!" Jill moaned.

"No, it's ok. I didn't see it at first but now it feels like we missed out on this great experience."

"You're right. That would have been so much fun!" Jill thought about it for a second then said, "Do you want me to get a divorce and start from the beginning so we can share that?"

They both started laughing.

"Yes. Yes, get a divorce and get married again but in a year so we can do all that." When they stopped laughing Megan added, "Of course, even if you did, it's not the same when you know the ending. And if he proposed again, really, how can you top Paris?"

"I know! It's a short story, but what a story!"

"I really am happy for you. I hope you know that."

"I do. And thanks for being so understanding." Jill leaned in to hug Megan and said, "I'm really glad you're here."

"Me too."

Jill leaned back and looked at what they had done so far. "We're coming along nicely and I really like this color. Let's take a break and eat something."

They walked into the kitchen, washed up and started to grab things to make sandwiches.

"I've got something else to tell you," Megan said.

"What?"

"Well, part of me was really mad that you went on the trip, then got married, then were moving to California and yet I couldn't be mad at you, so I convinced myself that there was this crazy conspiracy involving Jim and his friends."

"What?"

"About a year ago when you were breaking up with Jim, you told me some of the stories about his old college friends, the frat boys, and the pranks they'd play on each other. I just built this scenario in my mind that his friends came up with an elaborate prank to get him to marry you on a dare or something idiotic like that. When you first told me you got married I just couldn't believe that you really wanted to do that. So I figured there must be some other reason, like you were tricked somehow. I got this strange idea that, well… something like, Jim's friends dared him to marry you and he did it as a joke."

Jill chuckled, "That's funny." Then she became serious. "But you don't really believe that? Even if it was a trick I still had the opportunity to do whatever I wanted. I had my own ticket home and could have left at any time. I could have said no to the proposal or the idea that we get married right away. You know that, right?"

"Yes, now, but at the time I was overwhelmed and wasn't thinking straight."

"That is pretty funny."

"Well, it's funny now, but Jim's friend? The one that was here when we arrived?"

"Yeah, he's cute, don't you think?"

"Yes, but… I let him have it. I couldn't hold back."

"No!"

"All the anger, the crazy conspiracy stuff."

"No!"

"Yup, it all came out."

"Why?"

"Even after you told me you were married, and you packed everything up and we flew out here, I think I was in denial. When we were on the plane it was like we were going on another trip together and everything was still going to be the same as before. But as soon as I stepped into the house it hit me. All of a sudden it became so real, walking in the door, realizing this is where you were going to live, actually meeting your husband– hm, I think that's the first time I've called him that. Up to that point I could still deny it, but then I just panicked and I was mad and I lost it."

"When? You seemed fine."

"I bit his head off when we were outside and you and Jim stepped inside, and again when the guys got the suitcases and we were in the bedroom."

"No! What did he say?"

"At first not much then he said that if there was a conspiracy it was between you and me, and how did he put it? Oh yeah, we concocted a plan to," she spoke slowly, "snag a husband with a carefully laid Man Trap."

They both laughed so hard they could barely remain standing.

When Jill caught her breath she said, "So was this Man Trap like those traps they use at national parks to catch troublesome bears?"

"I've never seen those."

"They're like a big cage with a huge, juicy steak hanging in the middle. And when they grab the steak, GOTCHA!"

They laughed for a long time, then Jill said, "Well, we'll just have to see if we can fix this."

7

The next day, Friday, I walked into work around 1:00 in the afternoon.

"Where have you been all day," Jim asked.

"At the printer's. The file didn't RIP correctly and I spent most of the morning figuring out it was a bug in the newest version of the design software we use so it took awhile to come up with a workaround. I've got to head back in a little while for a press check, something that should have happened this morning, so it's been a crazy day."

Jim leaned back in his chair, put his feet up on his desk and smiled, "It sucks to be you."

I stop what I'm doing, turn toward Jim and fold my arms across my chest. "Yes, I guess it does. So how is it going with the additions to the R.K.S. account? What about those extra software features that were promised?"

Jim takes his feet off of the desk and spins around. "It sucks. I told you management promised these new specialized features, right? Well to code this stuff is going to take about three times longer than promised. I've been trying to call in some favors to get extra programmers on it but everyone is booked. So now I have to look like the idiot and tell the client they're not getting the new features when they were told."

"Well, looking like an idiot is something you excel at so at least there won't be a problem there."

"Ha, ha. Tell me something. How is it that you're set up in here, in sales, with the exceptional employees?" Jim said glancing at his three, Salesman of the Year, trophies.

"Just marveling at your good luck, are you?"

"I… If it…" Jim sighed, "Yeah, you're alright."

"You couldn't think of a good comeback? You've been married how long, and your brain is turning to mush already?"

"It doesn't… I'm just…" Jim gives up and with a steely look and a monotone voice, says, "Don't make me call my wife and tell her you're being mean to me."

We both burst out laughing.

"There you go. That was a good one."

I grab my briefcase and sort through the contents making sure I've got what I need to head back to the printer later. "So have the girls redecorated your whole house yet?"

"Yeah, they're making a mess of it. By the way, I hope you don't have plans for dinner because I've been instructed to bring you home tonight."

I stop what I'm doing and look at Jim. "Oh, I don't think I can make it."

"Then you have to call Jill and tell her, I'm not. Besides, it was Megan's idea. I think she's hot for you."

I laughed. "No, not even a little. In fact she thinks this whole thing was my idea."

"What thing?"

"She thinks there was some kind of conspiracy to get you to propose to Jill. That your friends, with me as the ring leader, tricked you into thinking it was a good idea to propose and get married in Paris. And we're all laughing as if this is the ultimate prank– that we were able to trick you into getting married, and Jill is the unlucky benefactor of our cruel joke. And here's the kicker, Megan's furious about it, said she was going to kill me."

"What? You couldn't have known because even I didn't know what was going to happen."

"That's basically what I told her."

Jim paused, contemplating the implausibility of something like this. "Wow, she's a real loon." Then he smiled, "You two would get along just fine."

"Ha, ha. I'm not the one who flew to Paris on a whim and proposed to an old girlfriend I hadn't seen in over a year."

Jim stared off as if he were seeing what he did from a different perspective. "Now that you put it that way, it does sound a little crazy."

"No, not at all. People do that kind of thing all the time."

Jim shrugged, "Yeah, I guess so."

"No! It's totally crazy!"

"And this from the guy who hasn't been on a decent date in, what, three years? And who isn't happily married."

"Go ahead, act smug now. We'll see who has the last laugh."

"Alright, cuz I'm laughing so hard I think it's going to last for the rest of my life, even if I live until I'm a hundred."

"Fine."

"Fine. Then I'll see you at my house for dinner."

I stood there not wanting to go but thinking that if Jim and Jill were there then Megan wouldn't lash out. I just had to make sure we weren't left alone. "Yeah," I said resignedly.

I arrived on time, we made some small talk then ate right away, so things were going well. In front of Jim and Jill, Megan was pleasant if not very talkative. We finished dinner when Jill said, "Jim, can you help me in the kitchen for a second?"

"With what?"

"Some things."

I started to panic with the idea of being left alone with Megan. "I can help you Jill, I'd be happy to," I said.

"No, you're our guest," Jill said as she reached out and put her hand on my shoulder as if she was going to push me down if I got up.

"Oh, it's no trouble at all," I said as I pushed my chair back a little.

"NO," she said firmly. Then looked at Jim, smiled and said, "Jim will help me?"

"With what?"

"I need you to help me with *some things* in the kitchen," she said slowly with a frown on her face while gritting her teeth.

Jim finally got the message, then realized he was leaving Megan and me alone. As he grabbed two of the empty plates, he leaned in toward me and in a low voice so that Megan couldn't hear, said, "I heard her nickname is, barracuda." Then pulled back and twisted his head slightly as if to say, Good luck, before walking into the kitchen.

I was sitting across from Megan, squirming a little and trying to avoid eye contact. I envisioned her mouth unhinging like a cobra, as she rose up to bite my head off. She must have noticed my apprehension.

"I just wanted to apologize for my behavior the last time we met. It was rude and inappropriate, I'm sorry."

"Ok." My guard was still up, but Megan looked embarrassed and uncomfortable. "So you don't want to kill me? Or you do, but you won't?"

Megan smiled slightly. "No, no killing."

It looked like she wasn't going to provide any more information so I said, "Can I ask why you think it was a prank and I'm responsible?"

"I don't. I mean I did, but…" Megan sighed and then went into a lengthy explanation that lead up to the point when I first saw her. I had no idea she appeared reserved and shy because she was in shock.

"To deal with it, I was denial, but at that moment I couldn't push it away anymore, and fully realized that Jim was her husband and this was her house. This was where she was going to be spending her time, not with me, not in Chicago."

Megan wrinkled her nose, "And it was a pretty ugly house." We laughed.

"Me, I especially liked the display of authentic looking medieval swords, crossed, behind a shield with a coat of arms etched into it. Did that end up in the trash?"

"No, we turned that room that was filled with clutter into an office for Jim and put it in there, but if it were up to me, I would have thrown it in the trash." We chuckled.

Megan went back to her explanation. "So when I had the meltdown and yelled at you it was because I just couldn't let myself believe that Jill had willingly chose to marry Jim, and I came up with the only thing that made sense to me, that it was a trick. Does that sound crazy?"

"Not really. Not any more crazy than going to Paris on a whim and getting married."

"So on the crazy scale I'm not a 10, just an 8?" Megan said with a smile.

"Acting out, under extreme duress, is not crazy. Overall, maybe a 4, and I'm a 5 myself, so I can't hold that against you."

"From what I've seen, I would have a hard time believing you are a 5, but it's nice of you to say that."

As if she was the odd person out, the only one who thought this way, Megan asked, "Is it me or are the circumstances of this whole situation between Jim and Jill strange?"

"Strange is rather mild. I might add: bizarre, freakish, odd, crazy..." We both chuckled.

I went on, "I haven't known Jim that long, but I do know he can be impulsive. Still, it wasn't just odd when he told me, it was also that he didn't see anything unusual about it at all. He made up his mind that he was going to get married and the only thing left was the execution of his plan, and the sooner the better. It's one of the things that makes him a great salesman, he can focus without emotion or distraction. It's admirable, but also abnormal."

"He does seem like a nice guy, though, and Jill is very happy." Megan smiled, then mocking herself with a frown on her face, said, "So if your jerky buddy isn't good to her..." and we both laughed.

"Oh, I talked to Jim about Jill being his third choice, too. He admitted his first two were impulsive and not well thought out. The way he talked about Jill, it seemed like if he would have given it the thought it required, she would have been the first choice, by far."

"I think she's pretty special so the idea that she was third really bothered me. That's good to hear."

"I told Jill about what you said, that we were the ones who concocted a, "...carefully laid Man Trap." She asked if that was like those traps they use at national parks to catch troublesome bears."

I chuckled, "That's not a bad idea. You guys might be able to make some money off of that one."

"Yeah, we got a good laugh out of it." Megan paused then said, "So, I'm sorry. Do you accept my apology?"

"Yes, of course."

I changed the subject and asked Megan about Chicago, then her job, and she went on for a while. Jim and Jill were gone for a long time, as if they were making dessert from scratch, which was fine because it gave me some time to get to know Megan better.

In the kitchen Jim says in a low voice, "How long do we have to stay in here? They're laughing, so things must be going well."

"Just a second longer." Jill smiled, "I wanted to give Megan some time to set up her Man Trap."

"What?"

"Never mind. Let's go. Grab the coffee."

8

I show up at Jim's the next day, Saturday, in the evening. Jill answers the door, "Oh, come in. I'll go get Megan."

Jim is in the backyard, sees me and comes inside. "What's up?"

"They didn't tell you? I'm taking Megan out."

"Hey, good for you. That's great. Now don't try to break my record for shortest engagement."

"That's not a record I want to hold."

"Good, cuz I'm having a little plaque made. By the way, do you have protection?"

"Nothing is going to happen."

"Yeah, first date. Megan's a nice girl. But if you wanted to keep her out, like all night, that would be great because this will be the first time since they got here that Jill and I will be alone."

"So you're saying you're going to owe me one?"

"Well, I didn't say that…"

"Because we could just hang out here and get a pizza."

"Ok, ok. We'll just see when you guys come in." Jim looked over to the hallway that leads to the bedrooms. In a lower voice he says, "Hey, Jill made reference to a Man Trap? Do you know what that's about?"

"Yeah, I'll explain later."

Jill and Megan come down the hall and walk into the living room. Jim turns to me and says in a loud voice, "Now the rule is, she's got to be in by 11:00," winking so only I could see.

We all chuckle. "Oh Jim," Jill says, "Now you two just have a good time."

Megan and I head downtown. It's a great summer evening. We take a leisurely walk past a series of bars and restaurants with live entertainment. We stop for a drink and listen to a jazz trio, then move on to a gravelly-voiced lounge singer performing classics from bygone eras. Next, we have dinner at a nice restaurant on their outdoor patio, then continue exploring. A punk band commands our attention for a couple of songs, then we spend some time at another venue with a top 40 cover band, but without a place to sit, decide to move on. We find a long and narrow bar with dark hardwood paneling and the last booth in the back is vacant. There is a sultry jazz band up front we can't see, but the music softly filters back through the crowd. The waiter comes over and we order some drinks. He goes to get them.

"So you're going back to Chicago soon?"

"Yeah. I've got a flight back tomorrow."

I was having a good time. Megan was a lot more fun than I thought she was going to be, based on my first impression of her. "It's such a nice night, it reminds me summer is half over already and I haven't taken any time off yet."

"I've got a bunch of vacation time left myself."

"I was wondering…" I leaned in, looked into Megan's eyes and in a breathy, deep voice said, "Would you like to go to Paris with me?" There was a moment of silence then neither of us could keep a straight face. We both burst out laughing.

"No way!" Megan said as she shook her head back and forth.

I leaned back, still chuckling, "That was pretty funny."

"Oh, it was hilarious."

"I've really had a nice time tonight, it's too bad we couldn't spend some more time together."

"I would have liked that."

The waiter set our drinks down and Megan took a sip of wine, then pensively said, "I have an idea, if you are interested. I've lived in Chicago my whole life so I'm a pretty good tour guide. I can find you a great deal on a nice hotel and show you the tourist stuff plus all the great things the tourists never see, if you want to come out some time, before the end of summer."

"I'd love to, that sounds great. But wasn't Jill saying something about you going to Spain every year? For your vacation?"

"I've been there a lot, and I love Spain. But…" she stiffened her spine and in a low voice while rocking her head back and forth a little, said, "I'm changing it up. New woman," mocking Jim. We both laughed.

"There's always Paris," I said smiling.

"No. No way. I'm not going to Paris."

Back at Jim's house, most of the painting and decorating was done. The garage was filled with the overflow of the combined contents from Jill's apartment and Jim's house and if pressed, Jim would have to admit Jill and Megan had done a good job.

A warm breeze ruffled the curtains and moved through the house bringing the sweet smell of summer with it. Jim was in bed, rolled over on his back and exhaled heavily. "He shoots. He scores. Three times in one night. Hat trick, baby. High five." He held his hand in the air to his left. Jill was lying on her back next to him. She giggled and gave him a soft high five, then rolled over, put her arm around him and rested her head on his shoulder.

Jim was taking it all in. Brand new day.

"I love you," Jim said.

"I love you too, babe."